R0064979821

Maddox, Jake.

J
MADDOX   Whitewater courage

WHITEWATER COURAGE

BY JAKE MADDOX

ILLUSTRATED BY SEAN TIFFANY

text by Chris Kreie

STONE ARCH BOOKS
a capstone imprint

Jake Maddox books are published by Stone Arch Books
A Capstone Imprint
1710 Roe Crest Drive
North Mankato, Minnesota 56003
www.capstonepub.com

*Library of Congress Cataloging-in-Publication Data is available on the
Library of Congress website.*

Library Binding: 978-1-4342-2530-6

Summary: Christopher has never rafted on a river like the Australian
Franklin River. Will he be brave enough to tackle the whitewater?

Art Director: Kay Fraser
Graphic Designer: Hilary Wacholz
Production Specialist: Michelle Biedscheid

Photo Credits: Sean Tiffany (cover, p. 1)

Printed in the United States of America in Stevens Point, Wisconsin.
052012
006764R

TABLE OF CONTENTS

Chapter 1
WELCOME TO AUSTRALIA 5

Chapter 2
ON THE RIVER 9

Chapter 3
DOWNSTREAM............................13

Chapter 4
FIRST WHITEWATER.......................18

Chapter 5
KEEP DIGGING...........................22

Chapter 6
OVERBOARD 29

Chapter 7
THE RAPIDS 36

Chapter 8
IMPOSSIBLE 44

Chapter 9
LET'S DO THIS 50

Chapter 10
PICKING UP SPEED 54

Chapter 11
DANGEROUSLY CLOSE......................59

Chapter 1

WELCOME TO AUSTRALIA

Christopher Hawk and his sister, Sarah, walked down the long tunnel from the plane to the airport. Christopher stopped to look out a small window in the tunnel. The sky was a shade of blue he had never seen in Wisconsin.

"Look!" he said to Sarah. "We're really in Australia!"

"Cool!" Sarah said. "Come on. Let's find Uncle Nathan."

They followed the rest of the passengers into the gate. Christopher stared through the sea of people walking back and forth through the busy airport.

Soon, they found their uncle. Uncle Nathan hugged them. "I bet you're tired," he said.

"Yeah," Christopher admitted. "We left Wisconsin more than thirty hours ago."

"Let's get your bags and get out of here," said Uncle Nathan.

They walked through the airport and down the escalators to the baggage claim area. "How are your parents?" asked Nathan. "I bet they were nervous about sending you to Australia by yourselves."

"Mom was cool with it," said Sarah. "But Dad was freaked out."

Uncle Nathan laughed. "He's just worried because I'm his brother," he said. "Your dad still thinks I'm ten years old."

Christopher and Sarah grabbed their bags from the luggage carousel. Then the three of them walked outside to Nathan's truck.

"We're going to have a great time in Tasmania," Uncle Nathan said.

"We're going rafting down the Franklin River, and then we'll spend a week at the beach," said Sarah. "Right?" She was bouncing in her seat with excitement.

"That's right," said Uncle Nathan. "We'll camp next to the river tonight and start our rafting trip tomorrow." He looked over at Christopher. "Are you okay, buddy?" Uncle Nathan asked.

"I read that the Franklin River is really high because of all the rain recently," Christopher said. "Some people canceled their trips. They said other people should stay off the river."

Sarah rolled her eyes. "Christopher is pretty scared," she said. "He doesn't think we should go on the rafting trip."

"I'm not scared," said Christopher.

"It's okay," said Uncle Nathan. "I wouldn't take you on this trip if it was dangerous. You're safe with me. Besides, you might not make it back to Australia for a long time. You don't want to miss this chance."

"I know," Christopher said.

"Then our next stop is the Franklin River!" said Uncle Nathan.

Chapter 2

ON THE RIVER

The next morning, Christopher, Sarah, and Uncle Nathan stood on the banks of the Franklin River. The raft was inflated, the gear was loaded, and they were nearly ready to go.

"Help me tie down these bags," said Uncle Nathan. He was holding a handful of cords.

"Why do we have to tie the gear down?" asked Christopher.

"In case the raft tips over," said Sarah. "Right, Uncle Nathan?"

"Right," said Uncle Nathan. "Or in case a big wave of water hits the raft. We don't want our gear flying into the river."

"Wait a second. The raft might tip over?" asked Christopher.

"It might," said Uncle Nathan. "But we'll have life jackets and helmets on. Nothing's going to happen to us."

As he helped Uncle Nathan tie down the gear, Christopher looked at the truck. "What are you going to do with your truck?" he asked.

"A couple of my friends are going to drive it downriver," said Uncle Nathan. He finished tying the last bag. "My truck will be waiting for us."

"Let's go, guys!" said Sarah. She could hardly contain her excitement.

"Okay," said Uncle Nathan. "Hop in!"

Sarah and Christopher climbed into the raft. Sarah sat on the right side, and Christopher sat on the left. Uncle Nathan gently pushed the raft into the river. Then he jumped in. He sat in the back of the raft so that he could steer.

"Here we go, guys," said Uncle Nathan. "Get ready for the trip of a lifetime."

Chapter 3

DOWNSTREAM

Once they were on the river, Christopher
didn't feel as nervous. The sun was shining,
and the water was peaceful. He took out his
Southern Australia Wildlife Guide.

He paged through the book, stopping
to look up and check for real-life examples
of the animals inside. "Hey, that's a Green
Rosella," he said, pointing up into the trees.
"See the green and yellow bird?"

"Yeah, I see it," Sarah said.

"And look, way up there on that mountaintop," said Christopher. "My guidebook says those pine trees are more than three thousand years old."

"Cool," said Uncle Nathan. "I've been living here for ten years, and I didn't know that."

The group enjoyed the scenery as they floated lazily down the river.

"Around this corner, there's a giant tree that hangs over the water," Nathan told the kids. "It's something I always look for. You can tell how high the river is by how far it goes up the tree's trunk."

The raft floated around a bend in the river.

"Whoa," said Uncle Nathan.

"What?" asked Christopher.

Uncle Nathan pointed to the left bank of the river. "Over there," he said.

"I don't see anything," said Christopher.

"That's the problem," said Uncle Nathan. "You can't see it. The tree is totally under water. Usually it's a foot or two above the river."

"Wow," Sarah whispered. "So the river is really high?"

"Yes," Uncle Nathan said. "It's higher than I've ever seen it."

"What does that mean?" asked Christopher. He was beginning to get worried again.

"It means the whitewater is going to be bigger and faster," said Sarah.

"That's right," said Uncle Nathan.

"Are we going to be okay?" asked Christopher. His voice was shaky.

"We'll be fine," said Uncle Nathan. "I'll make sure of it. Now it's time to get your helmets on, guys. Our first whitewater is coming soon."

Chapter 4

FIRST WHITEWATER

Christopher's heart raced. Suddenly, he could hear the sound of loud, rushing water.

"This stretch of whitewater should be pretty easy," said Uncle Nathan. "It's not very big, so it'll be good practice for the more difficult stuff later."

The raft picked up speed as the river narrowed. Water bubbled up and over rocks that stuck out of the river.

Uncle Nathan steered the raft through the rocks as Christopher and Sarah pulled their paddles through the water. The raft bobbed up and down on the waves.

Christopher could see a small waterfall ahead. Uncle Nathan steered the raft straight toward it. Quickly, the raft fell two or three feet. A wave of water washed over the raft, soaking Christopher and Sarah.

"Yee-haw!" shouted Sarah.

Christopher smiled. He was still scared, but he was having fun. Rafting through the whitewater reminded him of water rides at an amusement park.

After several more waves and a couple of sharp turns, the group found themselves in quiet water once again.

"That was awesome!" shouted Sarah.

"What did you think, Christopher?" Uncle Nathan asked.

Christopher turned and looked back at his uncle. Then he smiled and gave two big thumbs up.

Chapter 5

KEEP DIGGING

Christopher, Sarah, and Uncle Nathan paddled their raft down the Franklin River for several more hours. They passed through a few more stretches of whitewater. After each one, Christopher felt more confident. Soon, he wasn't scared at all.

After a while, the sun started to sink lower in the sky. "See that large flat rock up ahead?" Uncle Nathan said, pointing. "That's where we'll land for the night."

Once they'd paddled the raft to the rock, Christopher and Sarah hopped out. They unpacked their gear and set up the tent while Uncle Nathan started a fire and made dinner.

After they ate, Uncle Nathan stood up. "We should get to bed," he told them. "We need to be rested and strong. Tomorrow we'll be going through some really big whitewater."

"Bigger than today?" asked Christopher.

"Yes," said Uncle Nathan. "But you can handle it. You'll be ready."

"If you say so," said Christopher.

* * *

The next morning, Sarah and Uncle Nathan were sitting by the fire when Christopher crawled out of the tent.

"Come and get some breakfast," Uncle Nathan said, stirring a packet of instant oatmeal into a bowl of hot water. "It's 6:30 now. I'd like to be on the river by 7."

After breakfast, Christopher and Sarah rolled up their sleeping bags and packed their backpacks. Uncle Nathan took down the tent and strapped all the gear into the raft.

They were on the river by 6:55.

"We're ahead of schedule," Uncle Nathan said, checking his watch. "Good work, team. Whitewater, here we come."

"Awesome!" Christopher said. He felt ready to take on the whitewater ahead.

They spent the morning paddling through several stretches of rapids. Sarah even took a turn steering the boat.

Just as Christopher started to wonder when they would stop for lunch, a shout came from the back of the raft.

"Okay, helmets on!" yelled Uncle Nathan. "We're coming up to the big whitewater."

As the raft turned a corner, Christopher gasped. Ahead of them was the most violent stretch of river he'd ever seen. Huge waves crashed over giant boulders. Water rushed rapidly between the rocks. Whirlpools circled among the rapids. "This looks pretty crazy," Christopher said.

"It'll be okay," said Uncle Nathan. "We can do this. I promise."

As the river began to speed up, Christopher dug his paddle into the water faster and faster. Sarah did the same thing.

In the back, Uncle Nathan steered the raft between the boulders and over the high waves.

As the raft shot forward, Christopher felt helpless. The river was moving them along. He kept reaching his paddle into the water, but it seemed pointless. He didn't feel like his paddling was doing anything. The river was in total control.

"Keep digging!" yelled Uncle Nathan. "Keep digging!"

Christopher did what he was told. Over and over, he plunged his paddle into the river.

Suddenly, the raft crashed headfirst into a tall wave. For a brief moment, the raft didn't move. Then, slowly, it began turning sideways.

Christopher knew it was bad for the raft to turn that way. He knew that it was important for them to go through the rapids in a forward direction. Going down the river sideways meant danger.

"Hang on!" yelled Uncle Nathan.

Christopher held onto his paddle with one hand. With his free hand, he grabbed the strap next to his leg. The strap would keep him in the raft if it turned over or crashed.

Sarah kept paddling. "Hold on!" Christopher told her. But she didn't listen.

The raft slammed sideways into another wave. Sarah was thrown overboard.

Chapter 6

OVERBOARD

Sarah bobbed up and down in the whitewater. Christopher could see the panicked look in his sister's eyes. She tried to reach the raft, but the river pushed her away.

"Don't fight it!" yelled Uncle Nathan. "Just relax your body!"

Christopher didn't know what to do. He fought to keep his eyes on his sister. The raft sped down the river.

Several times, Sarah disappeared from Christopher's view. Each time, he worried that he would never see her again. Sarah was floating further and further from the boat.

"Aren't you going to do anything?" Christopher yelled at his uncle. "We need to jump in after her!"

"It wouldn't do any good," Uncle Nathan said. "There's no way we could get to her in this water. But we're almost through the whitewater. She's being pulled through the whitewater too, and once we're all through, we'll be able to reach her."

"It's almost over, Sarah!" shouted Christopher. "Just stay calm!"

Soon, the water calmed down again.

"Let's go," said Uncle Nathan. "Paddle!"

Christopher and Uncle Nathan quickly paddled toward Sarah. In the calm water, they reached her easily.

Uncle Nathan reached over and scooped Sarah into the raft. "Are you okay?" he asked, hugging her.

"I'm fine," said Sarah. "That was wild."

"Are you sure you're okay?" asked Christopher. "You scared me to death."

"I'm sure," said Sarah. She smiled. "Really, I'm fine. It was scary, but I knew you guys would save me."

"Let's get off the river for a little while," Uncle Nathan said.

The group paddled the raft to shore. Christopher was the first one out. He was so angry that his whole body shook.

"You said you were going to keep us safe!" he shouted, staring at his uncle. "Sarah almost died back there."

"I didn't almost die, Christopher," said Sarah. "I'm fine."

"Try to stay calm," said Uncle Nathan. "When you raft through whitewater, you sometimes end up in the water. It's normal. That's why we wear helmets and life jackets."

"I don't know if I can do this anymore," said Christopher. He felt his face heating up.

Uncle Nathan put his arm around Christopher. "I can't promise what happened to Sarah won't happen again," Uncle Nathan said. "But I can tell you you'll be okay."

"Can't we just turn around and go back?" asked Christopher.

Uncle Nathan shook his head. "No, we can't," he said. "That's impossible."

"We'll be fine, Christopher," said Sarah. She gave her brother a hug.

"We can do better next time if we paddle the correct way and use the right techniques," said Uncle Nathan. He shot Sarah a glance and added, "And if we follow safety directions all the time." Sarah turned red and nodded.

"So what do you say, Christopher?" Uncle Nathan asked.

Christopher looked at the river. He wondered what big rapids were waiting for them downstream. "I'm not sure," he said finally.

"We're depending on you," Uncle Nathan said. "Sarah and I can't do this alone."

"You can do it," said Sarah.

Christopher took a deep breath. "If you need me," he said, "I think I can do it."

"Great," said Uncle Nathan. "Let's do this."

Chapter 7

THE RAPIDS

After lunch, the group was back on the river. Christopher still felt really nervous. He knew they were getting close to the biggest whitewater they would face during the entire trip.

"Here we go, guys!" shouted Uncle Nathan.

"Let's do it!" said Christopher. He was trying to build up his courage. But inside, he was terrified.

The speed of the water picked up. The raft flew down the river. It dipped up and down over the big waves. Water spilled over Christopher's feet.

Uncle Nathan shouted instructions. "Christopher, dig!" shouted Uncle Nathan. "Sarah, relax!"

Christopher reached deep into the river with his paddle. He pulled it quickly through the cool water, then back up again. Sarah held her paddle in front of her.

Uncle Nathan had taught the two of them to listen closely to his instructions. When he yelled "dig," that meant they should paddle as hard as they could. When he yelled "relax," that meant they should stop paddling.

Uncle Nathan had said it was important to know when to paddle and when not to paddle. That would keep the raft heading straight down the river.

"Okay, both of you," shouted Uncle Nathan. "Dig!"

Christopher and Sarah paddled as hard as they could. The raft kept a straight course down the river.

They were going fast, faster than they had ever gone before. Christopher wondered what would happen if the raft suddenly hit a huge rock. He shook his head and tried not to think about it.

"Sarah, dig! Christopher, relax!" Uncle Nathan called.

Christopher lifted his paddle out of the water and waited.

He looked back at Uncle Nathan. His uncle's paddle was in the water behind the raft. He was using it to steer them through the water.

"Christopher, dig! Sarah, dig!" shouted Uncle Nathan. "We're coming up to the most difficult part!"

Christopher dug his paddle through the water. He waited for the next instruction. The water got rougher and rougher, and his heart pounded.

I hope I can do this, he thought nervously.

"Okay, you guys," Uncle Nathan called. "Relax, and hang on!"

Christopher grabbed for the strap by his foot. The raft shot through a narrow stretch of water, then fell four feet over a waterfall.

Suddenly, the raft slammed into a rushing wave. Christopher held on tight.

He looked over at his sister. This time Sarah was hanging on too.

The raft tipped back and forth in the rushing water. Then it was pushed sideways.

"I can't control it!" yelled Uncle Nathan. "Hang on!"

The raft spun around. Backward, it continued down the river.

"Dig!" Uncle Nathan yelled. "Both of you, dig as hard as you can!"

Christopher followed his uncle's instructions, even though it was hard to paddle against the current.

"Dig! Dig!" shouted Uncle Nathan.

Christopher and Sarah pulled their paddles through the wild river. Uncle Nathan tried to steer them forward.

It was working. The raft slowly turned in the rushing water. As Christopher could feel his hard work paying off, he pushed even harder.

The raft finally turned around. It shot forward through the rapids.

"We did it!" shouted Sarah.

"Yes, we did!" yelled Uncle Nathan. "But keep digging!"

Christopher kept paddling. *Is this whitewater ever going to end?* he thought.

After several more difficult minutes, it did. The raft was finally on quiet water again.

Christopher sank into the bottom of the raft.

"You did it, Christopher!" yelled Uncle Nathan. "You did it!"

"Wake me up in an hour," said Christopher. Uncle Nathan and Sarah laughed. Christopher smiled and closed his eyes. Every muscle in his body ached.

We made it, he thought. *We made it.*

Chapter 8

IMPOSSIBLE

Christopher woke up an hour later when he heard his uncle shouting.

"Hello!" shouted Uncle Nathan.

Uncle Nathan was waving to somebody on shore. A man standing on the riverbank waved back.

"Can we land?" asked Uncle Nathan.

"Yes, you can," said the man. "Bring your raft in."

Christopher and Sarah paddled the raft forward while Uncle Nathan steered them to shore.

"I'm John Henders. I'm surprised to see you folks on the water," said the man. He helped Christopher and Sarah out of the raft.

"Why?" asked Christopher, taking off his life jacket.

"Don't you know about the warnings?" John asked. "The river is very dangerous right now."

"Yeah, we heard," said Sarah. She smiled. "But our uncle is an expert rafter. Right, Uncle Nathan?"

"I've been on this river a lot," said Uncle Nathan. "And we've already gone through the toughest rapids. We're getting off the water tomorrow."

John frowned. "If you think you've gone through the toughest part of this river already, you're dead wrong," he told them. "Let me show you."

John pulled a river map out of his pocket and unfolded it. He laid it on the ground next to the campfire. "See this here?" said John, pointing at the map. "This is the landing."

"Yes," said Uncle Nathan. "I've landed there dozens of times."

"You've landed on a flat rock, right?" asked John. "Well, with the river as high as it is right now, that rock doesn't exist," he explained. "It's covered with water. Landing in that spot would be really hard for three adults. For two kids and one adult, it'll be next to impossible."

"So, if we miss it, we'll just land somewhere else downriver," said Sarah.

John looked at Uncle Nathan. They were both silent for a moment.

"If we miss the landing, we will drop into a deep ravine," said Uncle Nathan. "It has steep cliffs on either side."

"You wouldn't be able to get off the river for at least a mile," John told them.

"Could we just hike out from here?" asked Sarah.

"That would take days," said John. "Do you have enough supplies for that?"

Uncle Nathan shook his head. "No," he said. "We only have enough for the trip we planned, plus a little more for emergencies. I didn't plan for a four-day hike."

"What are we going to do?" asked Sarah.

Uncle Nathan took a deep breath. "I'm not sure," he told her.

Christopher cleared his throat. "I know what we're going to do," he said. "We're going to make the landing. We can do it. I know we can."

"I'm in," said Sarah.

"All right," said Uncle Nathan. "I guess that settles it." He looked at John. "Can you tell us about the landing?"

"I'll do the best I can," John said. "But the only way you'll make it is if you're a perfect team."

Chapter 9

LET'S DO THIS

Christopher had trouble sleeping that night. In his dreams, he was rafting over a waterfall that never ended. He kept falling and falling and falling.

He woke up sweating and couldn't fall back asleep. He climbed out of the tent as soon as the sun came up.

After packing their gear and filling their stomachs, Christopher, Sarah, and Uncle Nathan launched their raft.

They waved goodbye to John as they floated away from the campsite.

The sun was shining. Flocks of birds sang from the trees. The water was quiet. But Christopher still felt nervous. His sister and uncle were silent. He knew they were all thinking about the danger that lay ahead on the river.

After an hour or so, Christopher took out his wildlife guide and paged through it. "Sarah, did you know that in 1982 they almost built a big dam in this river?" he asked. "But some protesters stopped it from happening."

He flipped through some more pages. "And did you know that the Tasmanian Tiger Snake lives in this area?" he asked. "It's one of the top ten most poisonous snakes in the world."

"How can you be so calm right now?" Sarah asked. "Aren't you nervous about the whitewater?"

"Why do you think I'm reading this book?" asked Christopher. He laughed. "Of course I'm nervous."

"Do you really think we should try to land?" Sarah asked. "What if we miss it?"

"We can do it," said Christopher. "I know we can. I'm not worried."

Sarah shook her head. "You sure have changed since we started this trip," she said. "You were so scared before."

"Helmets on, guys!" shouted Uncle Nathan. "The landing is a few hundred yards ahead."

"Let's do this," Christopher said.

Chapter 10

PICKING UP SPEED

The raft picked up speed as the river narrowed. Christopher and Sarah dug their paddles into the water. The raft bobbed up and down in the rapids.

Christopher's heart was racing, but he tried to stay calm. He looked at his sister. Sarah's eyes were locked straight ahead.

"There's the landing!" shouted Uncle Nathan. "It's on the right, about two hundred yards up!"

Christopher spotted the tiny opening next to the river. It was the one spot on the edge of the river that wasn't lined with sharp boulders. The water rushed and foamed in front of it.

Christopher remembered what John had told them. Landing in that spot was going to be extremely difficult.

"We're going to angle in from the left," Uncle Nathan said. "When I say 'dig,' paddle as hard as you possibly can."

Uncle Nathan steered the raft to the right side of the river. Christopher and Sarah kept paddling. The raft bounced through the foam of the whitewater. Water sprayed up all around them.

Christopher waited for the signal from his uncle. He looked at his sister. Neither of them said a word.

The landing was getting closer and closer. He shut his eyes for a brief moment. *I can do this,* he thought. *We can do this.*

"Dig!" shouted Uncle Nathan.

Christopher opened his eyes.

"Dig!" Uncle Nathan yelled again.

Christopher took a deep breath. Then he punched his paddle into the river.

Christopher and Sarah pulled their paddles through the water. Christopher's muscles ached. But he ignored the pain. He paddled on.

"Dig! Dig!" Uncle Nathan yelled. He steered the raft toward the landing. They were just a hundred feet away. Christopher could see Uncle Nathan's truck waiting near the shore.

Christopher paddled. Sarah paddled. "Dig! Dig!" Uncle Nathan called.

The landing was close. In just a few seconds, Christopher would be able to reach out and grab a nearby tree branch that hung into the water.

Suddenly, Christopher felt a bump. The raft came to a quick stop. "What happened?" he asked.

"I think we hit a rock," Uncle Nathan said.

Christopher looked back at the shore. He could see Uncle Nathan's truck. The raft started moving away from it.

The raft picked up speed.

They had missed the landing.

Chapter 11

DANGEROUSLY CLOSE

Christopher heard a loud roar. It was the waterfall just ahead, he realized. The waterfall that would drop them into the deep ravine.

He scanned the riverbank. Tall, jagged rocks lined both sides of the river.

It would be impossible to land the raft on those rocks. The raft continued to shoot down the river. They were getting dangerously close to the waterfall.

Then Christopher spotted a large tree that hung over the river. The waterfall was just fifty feet past the tree.

"Look!" shouted Christopher. "Up there! If we can get to that tree, we can grab on to it. Then we can climb out of the river."

"It's worth a shot," Uncle Nathan said. "Good plan."

Christopher and Sarah began paddling hard. Uncle Nathan steered the raft toward the tree. They were moving fast. It was going to be a hard landing, but getting to the tree was their last hope.

"Here we go!" Uncle Nathan shouted. "Get ready to grab the tree!"

Christopher and Sarah dropped their paddles in the bottom of the raft. They both got ready for the collision.

Thud! The raft slammed hard into the tree and stopped. Christopher and Sarah reached their arms around one of the tree's thick limbs.

"Climb out!" shouted Uncle Nathan. "Hurry!"

"What about the raft?" asked Christopher.

"Forget the raft!" Uncle Nathan told him. "Just get out."

Christopher and Sarah struggled to pull themselves onto the tree. As soon as they were safely in the tree's branches, Uncle Nathan leapt onto the tree. But just as his feet left the raft, it slid away and shot down the river. Christopher and Sarah watched as the raft bounced over a tall, jagged rock and disappeared over the waterfall.

Uncle Nathan, Christopher, and Sarah scrambled off the tree and onto dry land. They lay on the shore, gasping for breath.

"That was crazy," Christopher said. "Totally crazy. I can't believe we made it."

"Wait until we tell Dad," said Sarah.

"Do you have to tell him?" asked Uncle Nathan. They all laughed.

Christopher sat up quickly. "Wait a second," he said. "What about the keys? They were in your backpack!"

Uncle Nathan sat up and reached into his life jacket pocket. He pulled out the truck keys and shook them in his fingers.

"I took them out of the gear this morning," he said. "I had a feeling I'd want to have them close."

"Let's go to the beach," said Christopher. "I want to windsurf, and snorkel, and go deep sea fishing."

"And go parasailing, and surfing, and rent kayaks," said Sarah.

"Will you let me rest for at least one day?" asked Uncle Nathan.

Christopher and Sarah looked at each other and smiled. "Okay, one day," Christopher said. "But then we get to have some fun. We deserve it!"

ABOUT THE AUTHOR

Chris Kreie lives in Minnesota with his wife and two children. He works as a school librarian and writes books in his free time.

ABOUT THE ILLUSTRATOR

When Sean Tiffany was growing up, he lived on a small island off the coast of Maine. Every day until he graduated from high school, he had to take a boat to get to school! Sean has a pet cactus named Jim.

GLOSSARY

COLLISION (kuh-LIH-zhuhn)—a crash

CURRENT (KUR-ruhnt)—the movement of water in a river

DANGEROUS (DAYN-jur-uhss)—likely to cause harm or injury; not safe; risky

DOWNRIVER (doun-RIV-ur)—in the direction of the flowing current in a river or stream

EXPERT (EK-spurt)—very skilled at something or very knowledgeable about a subject

INFLATED (in-FLATE-id)—expanded, full of air

RAFT (RAFT)—an inflatable rubber craft with a flat bottom

RAPIDS (RAP-idz)—a place in a river where the water flows very fast

SCENERY (SEE-nur-ee)—the natural countryside of an area

TECHNIQUES (tek-NEEKS)—methods or ways of doing something

WHITEWATER (WITE-wah-tur)—fast, shallow stretches of water in a river

DISCUSSION QUESTIONS

1. Was Christopher right to be worried, or do you think he worried too much? Explain your answer.

2. What was the scariest part of this book? Talk about it.

3. Did Christopher, Sarah, and Uncle Nathan do the right thing when they decided to try to make the landing?

WRITING PROMPTS

1. Christopher and Sarah visit their uncle in Australia. Write about a place you'd like to travel to. Why do you want to go there? What would you see and do there?

2. At the end of this book, Sarah, Christopher, and Uncle Nathan talk about their plans for the rest of their vacation. What do you think happens next? Write a chapter that extends the story.

3. Christopher had never been whitewater rafting before he visited Australia. Write about something you have never done that you'd like to do.

MORE ABOUT WHITEWATER RAFTING

Whitewater rafting has been getting more and more popular since the 1970s.

Using a special inflatable raft made of rubber or vinyl, rafters travel down a river over areas of whitewater. Whitewater is formed when water is moving so quickly that it begins to churn.

Whitewater rafting is fun and exciting, but it can be dangerous. Rafters need to make sure they follow safety guidelines and never attempt to raft on a river that might be too dangerous.

There are six classifications for rivers that can help rafters determine whether a river is difficult or easy to raft. The classifications go from I — which is easy — to VI, which is nearly impossible to raft. There are river databases available online so that rafters can find out a river's classification ahead of time.

No matter what classification a river has, if a rafter is on the water, he or she needs to wear a life jacket at all times. Rafters should also know how to swim. And according to the American Whitewater group, no rafter should ever attempt to whitewater raft alone. In fact, most groups should be at least three people. It is also important to have a first-aid kit and first-aid skills like CPR.

Before embarking on a whitewater rafting trip, rafters must make sure that their raft is safe. They should bring extra paddles and have their equipment inspected.

Whitewater rafting can make for an amazing, memorable outing or even a long vacation. But it's a dangerous sport. It should never be attempted without safety precautions!